FELIZ NAVIDAD

Two Stories Celebrating Christmas

Song lyrics by
José Feliciano

Pictures by
David Diaz

FELIZ NAVIDAD

Two Stories Celebrating Christmas

ISBN 0-439-51717-6

Lyrics and arrangement copyright © 1970 by José Feliciano. Used by permission from J&H Publishing and by special arrangement with Feliciano Enterprises and John Regna.

Illustrations copyright © 2003 by David Diaz.
All rights reserved. Published by Scholastic Inc.
SCHOLASTIC, CARTWHEEL BOOKS, and associated logos are trademarks and/or registered trademarks of Scholastic Inc.

Library of Congress Cataloging-in-Publication Data available
Reinforced Binding for Library Use

10 9 8 7 6 5 4 3 2 1   03 04 05 06 07

Printed in Mexico   49
First printing, September 2003

To my children, Melissa, Jonathan, and Michael, and to children everywhere who cherish the magic of Christmas and its traditions. May we always treasure these memories and find a place for them in our hearts.   — JOSÉ FELICIANO

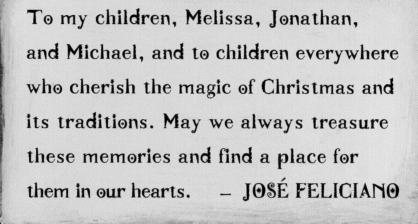

For D.L.S.

—DAVID DIAZ

**J**oin in the *parranda*, a long-standing Christmas tradition in Puerto Rico! During the holiday season, natives of this tropical island go caroling from house to house singing classic songs, called *aguinaldos*. *Los parranderos* get together and play instruments such as *guitarras* (guitars), *tamboriles* (small drums), and maracas to serenade a neighbor. The surprised neighbor invites *los parranderos* into their home for singing, dancing, and delicious food. But the party does not end there! The traveling party parades through the neighborhood, bringing the festivities to another house, then another, and another. This fun cycle of singing and dancing continues all night, as the party gets bigger and bigger with family and friends, young and old. At the last house, a huge outdoor cookout is prepared, complete with homemade foods and desserts and the typical *lechón asado*, or slow-roasted pig. This feast unites families, friends, and neighbors for a magical celebration during the Christmas season.

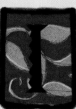

It is within the spirit of Christmas that family and friends come together to share the magic of this festive holiday. From winter wonderlands to warm tropical climates, people from every background celebrate the joy and beauty of Christmas. The essence of Christmas crosses all cultural boundaries as it sweeps people away in the excitement of parties, feasts, and celebrations around the world. Christmas trees and poinsettias, hot apple cider, and eggnog are just some of the classic traditions, but the real miracle of Christmas is in the power of giving and in the wonderful connections people make with each other around this enchanting holiday.

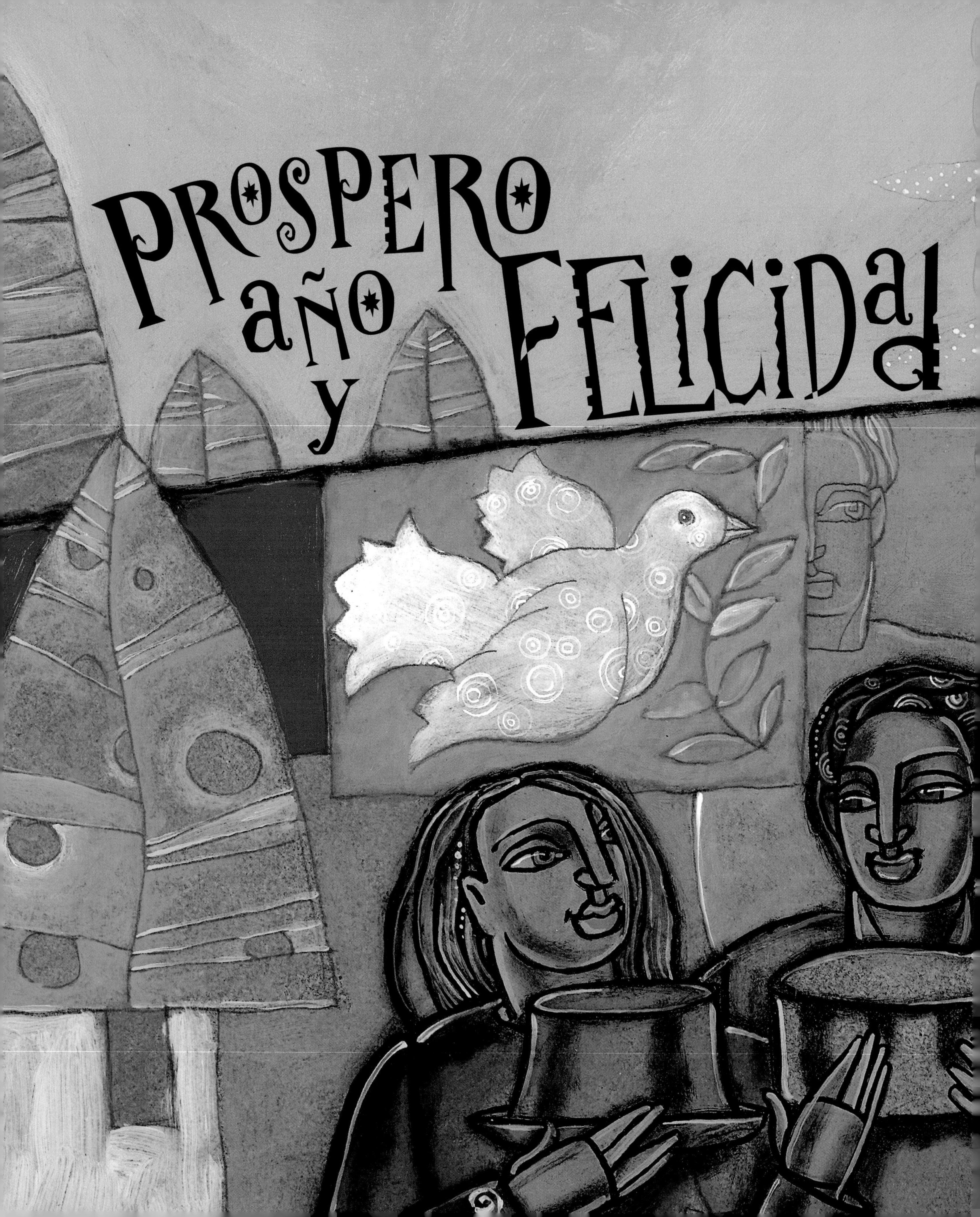
Prospero año y Felicidad

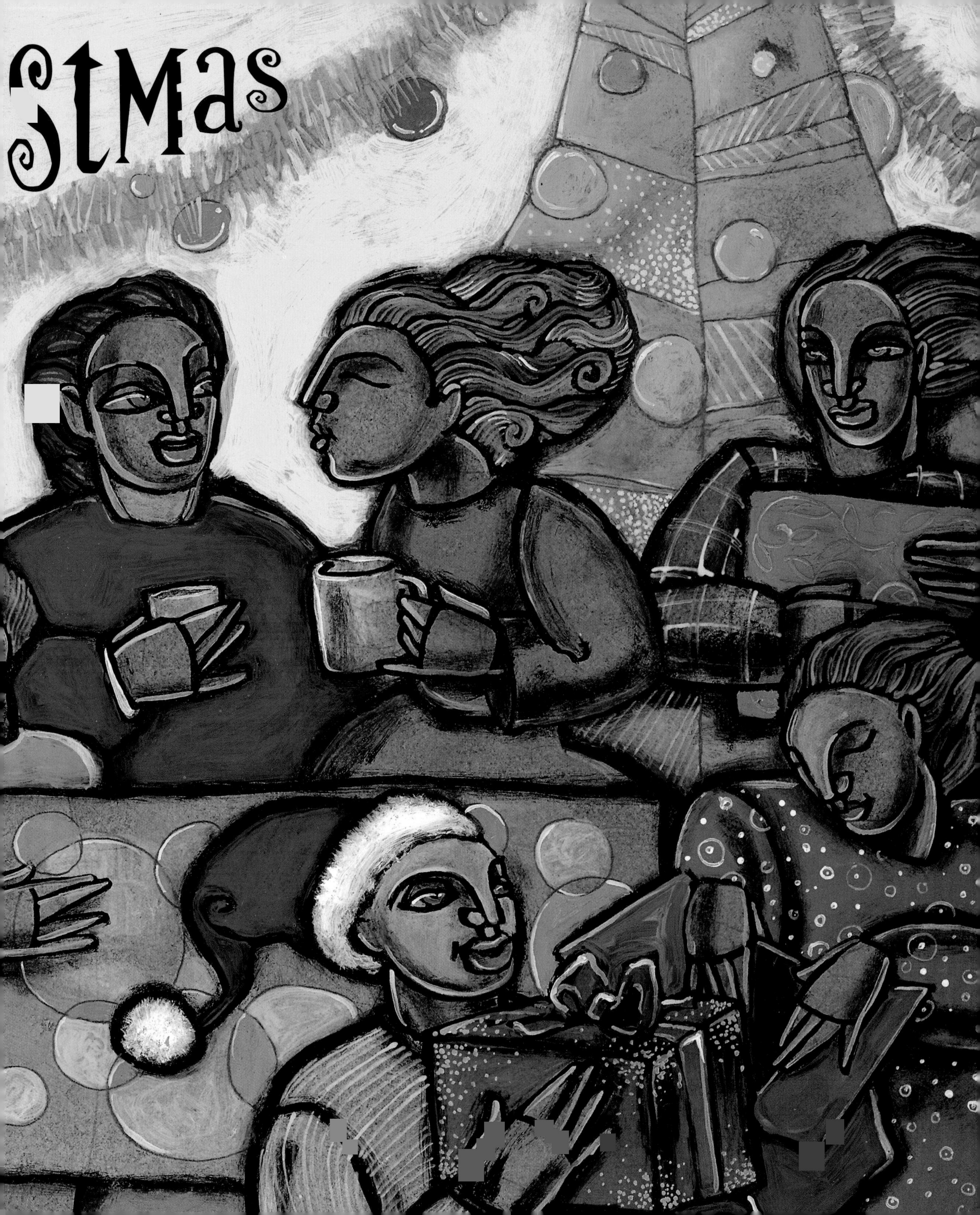
stmas